The Southern Concoction

JANNEKER LAWRENCE DANIEL

DEDICATION

This book is dedicated to the Lord, my God!

CONTENTS

ACKNOWLEDGEMENTS

Sincere thanks to my wife, for her understanding. Deep love for my daughter, who sacrificed much of her play time with me, so that I could pursue writing.

I thank my friend Ayan Pal, whose encouragement and insight made this piece of work possible.

I remember the constant and staunch support of my parents towards my writing endeavours.

I am indebted to my colleagues, students and friends for their constant support.

AUTHOR'S FOREWORD

Growing up under the tutelage of grandparents who could spin a yarn as well as anyone under the sun, I lived in two worlds; one of this world and the other of my own. Images grew monumentally. There was absolutely no limit to my imagination.

Then I stumbled across history, that of India. Rich is the history of India. Countless tales of courage, incredulity, tradition and innovation beg to be told to the outer world. The bedtime stories I listened to with rapt attention, the folktales I was regaled with by my friends in the village and the itch to write something... anything about India's past helped in some of the tales. I read history, heard history and when I wrote the same, it transformed into what you will read in this book.

THE BANANA LEAF

"How much longer should we carry this load? Are we anywhere near the place?" enquired the lanky American, cresting a slope.

"Us near caves" said the young boy in his limited English.

"How near? I am not able to see any signs" replied Anderson, peering through the mist down the lush valley.

"Far no. Very near caves. Me way know" said the boy, smiling to ease off the foreigner's anxiety.

Anderson grunted as he adjusted his rucksack and walked downhill after the nimble East Indian boy. The thoughts of the expectant little family made him hurry. He bumped into the boy who had stopped abruptly. The boy hunched down, motioned Anderson to do the same, went flat on his belly and slithered into the vegetation on his left. He joined the seated Anderson a little later.

"Bad people. Inform you" said Kai Lipong, the young boy.

After minutes of silence, the duo stood up and trudged towards their destination, a supposedly safe place. One had to be careful these days, thought Anderson, as the mission he was entrusted with concerned the lives of suppressed, stateless and hopeless families. He was to check if the caves shown by the boy were safe for the small Rohingya family. If so, hundreds of other families could be smuggled in.

Swathing their way through greenery atop towering

mountainsides, the American Human Rights Activist and Kai Lipong reached a small clearing in the forest that sprouted grass mounds. With a smile of reassurance, Lipong went to the grass mound farthest from them and edged his way along the cliff end on a narrow trail.

Anderson stood stock still, gaping with bated breath, the boy's agility. Lipong hugged the wall and inched his way onwards. He came to a yawning hole on the mountain wall and disappeared into it. Within a few seconds, he stuck his grinning face out of the hole and motioned Anderson to come. Anderson tightened his rucksack's strap and treaded towards the hole. After what seemed like the passing of an era, he climbed down the sanctuary of the hole, his breathing heavy.

What met Anderson's eyes was beyond his belief. Hundreds of natural caves ran down the length of the mountainous forest range near Devasora South, Mizoram, on the Indian side of the Bangladesh – India border. This was a discovery that could turn the course of the Rohingya refugees. He couldn't wait to take the news to his organization.

Kai Lipong gave his usual smile.

"All save people from Burma. Us good people" he said.

Anderson took the boy into a bear hug, evincing another infectious smile from the boy. Lipong went to the next cave and came with a can of water. Anderson accepted it gratefully and drank the nectar, feeling strength return to his tired limbs. They had a long walk ahead of them – to the Bangladesh border and beyond – as far as the Jadipai waterfalls. For near the waterfalls was the waiting family.

"Shall we go back for the family?" asked Anderson.

"I go India border. You go Bangladesh and get family" said Lipong and added, "I wait India."

"That's a good idea. I will bring them. Come, let's move" said Anderson, getting up.

Kai Lipong moved out of the hidden cave's entrance and became a human fly again, walking expertly from the side of the mountain to the wider space, and watched with bemused expression the American's dance of anxiety on the cramped pathway. Anderson's rucksack was now lighter as he had unloaded many items in the cave.

As they laboured through the thick forests, Anderson asked Lipong, "What are your parents? Where are you from?"

Lipong was silent, munching on a slice of pine apple that he had cut using a crude knife. Anderson knew better than to push him. It was a miracle that the boy was helping the refugees. Even governments refused to step in, warring with words instead, debating which side was right.

The prolonged walk was tiresome even for the hardy activist, who rested under a tree. Lipong hunched in front of him, offering two slices of the pine apple. As Anderson bit into a piece, Lipong said, whetting a twig with his knife, "Tiger kill mother. Father I not know. Live in church."

Anderson stopped crunching the fruit. He looked at the careworn face of the youth, hurriedly took out a twenty dollar bill and thrust it in his hands saying, "Use this after you leave me."

The boy's face gave way to a tired smile. He said, "I no want money."

Anderson kept his own counsel as he consumed the fruit slices. He asked him at last, "What do you want? Can I help you in any way?" When his organization gave him this mission, he was told that a boy named Kai Lipong would approach him at the Jadipai waterfalls in Bangladesh. He did not know anything else about the boy.

"Want hen in banana leaf" said Lipong.

"Hen? Oh… Chicken? You want to eat it on a banana leaf? That's it? That's all you want?" asked Anderson incredulously.

"I eat hen in plate. Church give one time. No eat hen in banana leaf" replied the boy.

"When we reach civilization, I will buy a chicken and a banana leaf" promised Anderson.

"Did they ever teach you English in the church?" he asked again, after a while.

"Yes. Me English good than others" smiled Kai triumphantly, his eyes twinkling.

As they reached the border, the American was again drawn by the beauty of the dense forests on both sides of the country. Mizoram's forest reserves seemed to be never ending. So impenetrable was the terrain there that it was normal for natives such as Lipong to cross between boundaries with ease.

Ajmal was shivering in the cold when Anderson spotted him.

Ajmal's sweater was worn by his wife in whose arms the one year old Faheema squirmed uneasily. Lipong was attracted to Faheema like a fly to honey. He offered to carry the little girl. Her mother refused graciously and politely. Not easily deterred, he continued his persuasion every few metres.

It was easier sneaking the family across borders than making progress in the forest. It was pitch dark when the group camped for the night. Lipong chose the place. There was a big tree that had its stem near a small boulder. The branches were so spread that the boulder was underneath. The fire lit by Lipong was between the small space near the rock and the tree stem. The rock reflected the heat from the fire, adding warmth and sheltering the fire from sudden gusts of wind.

The smoke from the fire went directly into the branches which dissipated the smoke, drawing no attention to the fire. Even Anderson who had been through many such expeditions found Kai Lipong to be extremely resourceful.

"I wake. No sleep. You sleep" said Lipong, pointing to the others.

"You will be tired Lipong. Let me stay watch. I cannot make you stay awake any longer" Anderson objected.

"I from forest. I no tired. You sleep" insisted Kai.

Ajmal, his wife Khadeeja and the infant were lying close to the fire, wrapped in blankets. Anderson hadn't realized how tired he was till he lay down on the moist earth. Before he could think further on his weariness, thoughts of his girlfriend Sally in Indianapolis transported him to America. He knew not when he drifted into a blissful sleep. He awoke with a start as a painful moan reached his ears. He almost screamed when something touched him on his hands. He turned to see Lipong bending over him.

"Ajmal cry in sleep. You go him" said Lipong, pointing his fingers at the bearded young man.

Anderson was about to move when Ajmal came up screaming. He hurriedly woke up Khadeeja crying, "They have come here. Come, let's run. Quick... Hand over Faheema to me."

Khadeeja came to herself, trying to placate her hysterical husband. She took a quick look at her sleeping child and asked Lipong to carry her out of earshot. Not needing to be told again, Lipong gently carried the sleeping baby and moved some paces away. Anderson was near Ajmal in a flash. He took hold of the young father and shook him.

"Ajmal... look, it's me Anderson. No danger here."

"Who? Who are you? Where is my child? My Faheema... Faheema... Khadeeja, where is our daughter?" Spotting Lipong in the distance with the little girl, Ajmal screamed his heart out and lunged forward brandishing a wicked looking knife in his hand, "Give me my child you treacherous cur. I will cut your heart out."

It took all that Anderson had to contain Ajmal. He pinned his arms and held him down as Khadeeja calmed him with soothing words. It took a couple of minutes before Ajmal broke down, tears streaming down his face. Khadeeja mouthed a 'sorry' to Lipong who smiled sweetly in return, handing over the still sleeping Faheema to her. Ajmal took the girl in his arms, gave a kiss of longing on her forehead and handed her back to his wife.

Ajmal turned to Kai Lipong who stood with his back against a tree. Still sobbing, he walked towards Lipong with outstretched arms. Both met, one with embarrassment and the other with gratitude of not having been slashed open with a knife.

The night was long. Except for the baby, the group sat huddled around the fire, sleep having fled them. Thick blankets wrapped around their figures kept the mosquitoes at bay. Lipong's hands kept shooing away insects and other measly looking little things that came flying near the sleeping child.

"We are not from Rakhine. We live… lived in the small town of Kawang in Mindat district. It is in the Chin state of Myanmar. No one knew we were Muslims. He was called Ohnmar. His parents had settled in Kawang forty years back" whispered Khadeeja, her eyes glued to the fire, her voice chillingly strange in the mountain.

Ajmal hooked his hands into his wife's hands and continued from where his wife left off.

"We had purchased a *tupi* for me the last time we visited Bangladesh. It fell out of my bag in the local bus when I was searching for a document. I hid it at once. I think somebody should've noticed. The Burmese military paid a visit to my house the very next day."

There was a sepulchral silence as Ajmal stopped. The faraway look on his eyes was interrupted by contortions of pain and anguish playing havoc on his handsome face. His body trembled. His lips quivered.

"We had gone to the market when a boy from the neighbourhood came with the news. I put my wife and daughter in the first truck that I could lay my hands on, to your organization" Ajmal said, looking at Anderson. He added, "I couldn't leave my parents and sister at home. I went home." He stopped, as images flooded his mind.

The sight of his father having been splayed across the wooden door of his backyard, the image of his mother's grey hair clotted in her own blood that had pooled around her caved-in skull... He shuddered. The most disturbing image was that of his sweet sister who had been studying in a university. She lay naked, her breasts slashed.

Ajmal couldn't bring himself to tell all these to his rescuers, nor ever to anyone. He wiped away his tears and turned to Lipong, "See... I am making all of you teary-eyed with my pathetic life. Do you know the meaning of my name Lipong? Ohnmar means 'mad.' I think with my Muslim name Ajmal, I will not have any more troubles. Ajmal means 'the most beautiful.' Nice name right?"

"Name good" said Lipong, his smile lighting up the mood of the group.

Dawn found the party on the Indian side, in the forests of Mizoram. They had to replenish their water supply. As usual Kai Lipong volunteered and went to a stream to fill their water canteens. There was a shout followed by an intense scuffling sound. Anderson was up in a second and moved towards the stream cautiously. Ajmal and Khadeeja crouched down instinctively, securing Faheema.

Two Burmese soldiers held Kai Lipong, who struggled to free himself of their vice like grip. Five more soldiers stood by. The leader, a middle-aged man sporting an unkempt beard of some days, sat on a small rock while his men stood near him. It was an uneven struggle, the little boy against the might of the trained soldiers.

"Is it this boy?" asked the leader.

"I think so. Let me check my Whatsapp" replied a soldier, poring into his mobile. His face brightened, and he showed a picture to the leader. It was of Lipong walking with Ajmal's family near the Jadipai waterfalls, Anderson in the background.

"Where are these people?" barked the leader.

"In Bangladesh. I come India" said Kai Lipong, not a bit frightened. The knowledge that he was in India strengthened him.

"Don't lie. They crossed the border. Where is the American?" asked the leader again, slapping him hard on the face.

Lipong reeled from the blow, blood flowing from his cut lips. He stood his ground, his usually gentle face defiant.

"Tie him to that tree" ordered the leader.

As soldiers tied Lipong to a tree, he wondered if this was an incursion. He as a civilian could sneak undetected across borders. But how did these soldiers come to India, in their uniforms?

Anderson had seen enough. He crawled stealthily back towards the family in hiding. Gathering their possessions they moved onwards to the caves.

"Can't we rescue him by any other means? Can you both do something? He's just a little boy!" pleaded Khadeeja.

"Nothing can be done. We must move before the men start searching the place" replied Anderson, making his voice gruff intentionally to stem the shakiness that threatened to down his voice. He had come to like the boy.

The journey to the caves was uneventful and silent, each one weighed down with speculations of what would've transpired in the interrogation of Kai Lipong. Anderson tied Faheema to his back using a blanket and walked on the narrow pathway to the cave. Khadeeja was persuaded to walk slowly, with Anderson coming back halfway to assist her and Ajmal bringing up the rear.

They had hardly settled in the cave when a young boy, a little taller than Lipong was, entered the cave.

"Kai?" asked the youth.

"Who might you be?" countered Anderson. Ajmal moved instinctively between the youth and his wife, a glinting knife in his hand.

"I friend Kai. Please… Please…" shouted the boy, alarmed at Ajmal's action.

Anderson moved beside Ajmal, patting his hand, "It's alright, Relax."

Ajmal brought down his hand, but stayed close to his wife and daughter.

"Sit down boy. What's your name? How do you know this place?" questioned Anderson.

"I Lei Tepong, friend Kai. Us find caves. Kai?" asked the handsome young man.

Getting no answer from Anderson, he persisted "Kai? Him life danger."

"Danger? How?"

"Burma soldiers ask Kai" said Tepong.

"But how did the soldiers get into this side?" asked Anderson.

"Usual" replied Tepong.

"Let's go and rescue Kai" said Anderson.

"Let me come with you" said Ajmal, getting up.

"No. If you die, the purpose for which we smuggled you across borders will go waste. Be with your family" said Anderson and moved out, with Tepong following him close behind.

When they reached the place, the men had left. Leftovers remained, of their food and of Kai, the gentle Kai. His legs had been smashed to pulp with the wooden logs that lay there, still smudged with blood. His hands were twisted in an unimaginable fashion, not possible when bones were intact. His face was untouched. He looked asleep. Tears had swept in torrents down his face.

His life had been snatched away by a long knife that protruded from his belly, as he lay sideways. The men had eaten a heavy meal before their departure and thrown the leftover near Kai.

And lying untouched near Kai was a fried chicken piece, on a torn banana leaf.

THE CROSS-OVER

Joe was a picture of anxiety as he walked to and fro on the corridor. It was past two thirty in the morning, but sleep was the farthest thing on his mind. He looked at his watch for the umpteenth time, wishing time would stop still. How he wished for his mother! His thoughts flew back to an incident that had happened fifteen years ago.

Joe had then been in his seventh grade. He had come home to see his father in a sour mood, staring moodily out of the window. He appeared not to notice Joe creeping noiselessly into the house. His mother placed a finger across her thin, pressed mouth and motioned Joe into the kitchen. As Joe tiptoed across the hall, his father looked up.

"Where did you go today?"

"I … I … went to school papa."

"Liar" shouted his father and lashed at Joe with an enormous hand, shaky due to alcohol.

The blow took Joe full on his jaw. He staggered across the room, falling heavily on the floor and breaking two of his teeth. Blood gushed from his nose. He lay whimpering as his mother rushed to his side. She took him to the backyard, hurriedly wiping the blood from his face and applying tincture on the broken skin.

"I went to school mummy. Honestly" he sobbed.

"I know my dear. I know. I know that you went to school. Now… do not cry" she said, wiping away the tears streaming down his face.

"Why is dad always hitting me mum?" sobbed Joe, looking up innocently at his mother who blinked back tears.

She asked Joe to lie down and placed his head on her lap. As he lay on her lap, she hummed his favorite song, petting his head simultaneously. Joe snuggled closer to his mother, secure in the comfort that she provided amidst the physical and mental pain prevalent in the house. As she kept humming, he drifted into a peaceful sleep.

Joe still remembered that incident. Though many such events happened thereafter, he never knew why *this* stayed fresh in his memory.

A sudden wail pierced his thoughts. He looked through the glass door which stood between him and his object of anxiety and anticipation. On a cot lay his wife, almost passed out by the exertions on her body. But her face looked angelic with joy. There was blood all about her. But her eyes were not on the blood or on her husband, but at her newborn son who was quacking like a duck in the hands of the nurse. The doctor having handed the baby to the nurse, walked out of the room patting Joe on the way, "He is a fine looking chap Joe. Looks fit to rule the world."

"Oh… ok doctor. Thanks a lot doctor" stammered Joe.

Joe held the infant ever so tenderly and gazed at his face. He was happy and proud, and was surprised to find tears roll out of his eyes.

Years passed by, and the love Joe had for his son grew monumentally. The child followed his father like a kitten following its mother. The affection between them was so obvious that Joe's wife could sometimes feel the green-eyed monster rearing its head.

It was in the boy's third standard that an event happened, that brought to light the level to which Joe was ready to go for the sake of his son. Joe was waiting for the school bus in which his son would come home. The yellow bus rumbled slowly through his street, turned the corner and stopped. The door opened and his little boy got down from the bus, into his open arms, weeping uncontrollably. The driver's assistant handed over the boy's school bag and the bus moved on. Joe was shaken.

"What's it son? What's the matter?"

There was no answer. The boy's cries increased.

"What happened Julian? Did anyone hurt you sonny?" pleaded Joe, as he walked home, with his son clinging on his shoulders.

Julian did not answer but cried his heart out. He did not open his heart to his mother either. The parents tried different methods to console their son, in vain.

Dinner was served. As was custom, Joe took Julian out for a walk before they went to bed.

"Look at that dog Julian. See how it is chasing its tail" said Joe, forcing a laugh and looking at Julian's face anxiously.

Julian clapped his hands in glee and watched the mongrel playing around in a mound of sand dumped for construction work.

"When can we have a dog of our own dad?"

"We are going to buy a dog tomorrow itself Julian. Which color do you like dear?"

"I want a brown fluffy dog with cute eyes… hmmm… dad, can we go and get one now?" asked Julian looking eagerly at his father.

"No buddy. Now the shops will be closed. We can go tomorrow and get *a brown fluffy dog with cute eyes*… happy?"

Julian nodded his head excitedly. Joe steered Julian towards the park at the end of their street. They walked slowly as Joe picked up the conversation again.

"How was school today?"

Julian was silent for a while. He then blurted out.

"Jack takes my watch every morning and gives it only in the evening."

Joe understood why Julian had cried so much. The watch had been a birthday gift. Julian loved it as the apple of his eye.

"Who is Jack?" asked Joe.

"He is the driver's assistant. He plucks the watch as soon as I board the bus. He hits me if I do not give it to him dad. I am scared of him."

"He hit you? When?" thundered Joe.

"He hit me today dad."

"Do not fear him. I will deal with this. And… not a word about this to your mom. Ok?"

"Sure dad. Will keep mum about this before mum" winked Julian, and started running in the pavement that ran along the borders of the park. Joe guffawed and followed in mock pursuit.

Needless to say, the driver's assistant Jack, did not come to school for a week after that owing to ill health. It was reported that he fell down from a speeding car. Some said that he had actually been pulled down from the school bus by a masked man and beaten severely. No one knew for sure. But neither Julian nor his watch ever came under any threat again.

It was during Julian's eighth grade that Joe felt the difficulty of a parent. Julian came home depressed one day. He spent the evening sulking. Joe ignored it for some time. The silence became unbearable. He peeped into Julian's room. The kid was sprawled on the ground, staring at the ceiling.

"Hi buddy, care for a coffee?" asked Joe, attempting at what he thought was his best smile.

"No dad. Don't feel like walking out of this room now" he replied, looking at his dad. Seeing the dejected look on his father's face, he added quickly, "Why don't you join me here dad?"

Joe accepted the offer and sat in a cushioned sofa near the door. There was an uneasy silence in the room as they looked at each other for almost a minute.

"Am I different in any way dad? Am I not normal?" burst Julian. Tears threatened to cross the threshold of his eyes. Joe heard alarm bells going off.

"No darling. You are absolutely normal. Whoever said that you are not?"

"Many of the boys in my class make fun of me. They say that I am neither a boy nor a girl. I … I also…I also do not know how to behave in class dad" cried Julian. Joe lay down next to his son, hugged him close and remained still. He did not know how to comfort his son, nor himself. He remembered Julian's childhood. Julian had never used any of his toys. The toy cars and toy bikes were untouched. So were the male miniature Superheroes. Julian had preferred Barbie dolls. He adored them. Joe had not taken that seriously. He expected the choices to change as adolescence bloomed. Now that things were at this stage, he did not know how to handle this. Julian meanwhile sobbed himself to sleep on his dad's shoulders. Both dad and son lay on the floor for two hours, after which Julian stirred awake.

"Would it bother you if I did not go to school?"

Joe was silent.

"Dad… please answer me. Would it be fine if I dropped out of school?"

"Why would you have to do that my boy?"

"I am not sure if I can handle the boys and girls in class."

"Do the girls also trouble you?" asked Joe.

"Well… the girls… they don't like me actually."

"How do you know that? You are a handsome boy. How can girls not like you?" retorted Joe. Joe had always been immensely proud of the good looks that Julian had inherited from his mother.

"Dad, you do not understand. Since the boys make fun of me, the girls do not let me sit next to them. They do not like me at all" said Julian, exasperated.

"But my dear, why should you go and sit with the girls? Why don't you sit with the boys as is the custom in your school?" asked Joe, curious.

"I like to sit *only* with the girls, dad. I do not feel comfortable amongst the boys."

An incident that had happened in Julian's fifth grade flashed across his mind. It was the fancy dress competition. As soon as Julian mentioned the contest, Joe thought of various methods in which he could help his son participate. He wondered what role his son would prefer. He had a list which had the names of Abdul Kalam, Gandhi, Jawaharlal Nehru and Netaji. He went into a state of shock when Julian insisted that he would dress up either as Indira Gandhi or as Kalpana Chawla. Both Joe and his wife tried to dissuade him. They succeeded finally.

Julian dressed up as *Sarojini Naidu*.

"Is it ok to sit with the girls, dad? Julian's question brought Joe out of his reverie.

Joe did not reply. It was then that realization struck him like a hammer. His son Julian was perhaps not his *son*. Perhaps he was a cross-gendered child.

Oh my God! How am I going to handle this? thought Joe, as his mind was filled with a whirlwind of emotions. He thought of his neighbors and relatives.

"Please help me dad. I cannot sit with the boys and do things like they do. I … I even want to dress like a girl. The clothes I wear now feels oppressive" sobbed Julian.

"You go to sleep now. Tomorrow you need not go to school. I need time to think sonny."

Joe went directly to the house of his friend Martin who lived across the city.

"Hey! What a surprise! Come on in Joe" shouted Martin from the porch as he saw Joe parking his Land Cruiser on the driveway.

"Why are you so pale? Are you sick?" asked a flustered Martin, as he espied his friend's forlorn look.

"This is about a colleague of mine. He has a son who he thinks is cross-gendered. The boy behaves like a girl. He is shunned by his classmates. My colleague wanted to know how to treat him. Can you help?" said Joe without breaking a sweat.

Martin gave his friend a searching glance and said with a knowing look,

"It is best to leave the child to its ways and yet have a watchful eye on everything in its life Joe. It is important to make the child feel special. He/she must not feel left out. Socialization is very much essential."

As the years rolled by, Julian's preference began to change more visibly. He gave up men's clothes. His wardrobe was filled with cosmetics that any woman would vie for. He preferred being called Julie. Needless to say, he had no friends. He rarely went out of house as the neighborhood did not take kindly to his transition. He was the butt of all jokes and became the object of ridicule. Children were frightened of Julian and adults gave him a wide berth. Joe spent a fortune taking Julian to various counselors and psychiatrists, determined to change Julian's attitude.

Then he realized a fact.

Julian had the urge within him to behave like a woman. There was no point in taking him to various people, who were strangers, to ask them to help his son change. It was not his son who had to change. It was the world that had to change the way in which it looked at Julian. The changed perception must start at home, realized Joe. For Julian, this method of living was normal. Forcing Julian to behave and live like a man would be abnormal. The thought chilled Joe. Relatives would ask Joe if Julian became normal. Joe would maintain silence. His heart would beat erratically and his mind would scream in protest that it was they who needed to change, and not his son.

Julian approached Joe one morning.

"Dad, I would like to start a business."

"Ah, Julie! That's good news baby. What do you plan to start?" asked Joe delighted at the prospect of helping Julian find a footing in his life.

"You have to help me in this father. I have no idea which type of business will suit me."

"Hmmm… let's think about this. Change your dress and come. Let us have Uncle Martin's opinion"

Martin was the only soul that Julian trusted apart from Joe.

Joe's wife watched from the balcony as Joe backed out his new Hummer from the garage and waited for Julian. Julian was dressed in a black sari and his shoulder-length hair was let free. Joe's wife looked at Julian with disgust. She had stopped talking with Julian ever since she learnt that he was cross-gendered. Once, she had even tried to send Julian out of the house when Joe was not at home. When Joe heard of it through Julian many days after the incident, he was livid with rage. He threatened his wife with divorce and made it clear that Julian was his top priority. That put a harness on her activities towards Julian. Though she despised Julian, she was scared enough of Joe, not to show anything outwardly.

She could never understand how Joe could cope with this. They were the elite of the society. Joe had always been conscious of moving around only in the highest circles of the world ever since his business had boomed. He was the icon of fashion and synonym of power. She enjoyed the warmth of his richness and could move with the wives of the most powerful men in the country. Now because of Julian's condition, she dreaded meeting the rich women. She too did not want to be treated as an outcast by the society. She distanced herself as much as possible from Julian.

The Hummer growled to life and moved out. Joe had been watching his wife's malicious expression through the rear view mirror. He had hoped that his wife would change her behavior towards Julian as days passed by. Sadly, that never happened.

Martin listened to the idea proposed by Julian. He then looked at Joe and asked him,

"How many inefficient workers do you have in your company Joe?"

"That would be around a thousand."

"Are you ready for a trip Julie?" asked Martin, grinning at Julian.

"Sure uncle. I am ready as I am."

"Hey guys, what are you talking about? Am I included or not?" asked Joe looking at Martin and Julian.

"You can come if you are interested" said a sober faced Martin, suppressing a grin.

"Interested? My foot! You bet I am!" exploded Joe, causing Julian and Martin to burst into loud guffaws.

The trio boarded the next plane to Mumbai, one of the cities with a heavy concentration of cross-gendered people without proper jobs. Mumbai became alive with an advertisement printed in almost all newspapers. An agency promised jobs for cross-gendered people and had scheduled interview in the next two days. Four hundred candidates were given offer letters and asked to report in Chennai the next month. The elated selection committee flew around the country picking up cross-gendered employees.

Julian became the Director of Joe's company. Notice termination with a time frame of six months was sent to almost a thousand employees who were competitively inept. The new candidates were categorized according to their educational qualifications. The segregation was an eye-opener for Joe and Julian. They realized how many cross-gendered people had been forced into drug dealing, prostitution and begging solely because of their gender.

Julian trained the new candidates. The energy of the candidates was amazing. The knowledge that they too were loved and accepted by the society made them joyous. They were crazy about Julian, their hero and emancipator. The Indian media went wild with news of this phenomenon. Julian received accolades from all quarters for the bold step that brought life and hope to millions of cross-gendered people in India.

It was a bright morning a year later, when Martin visited Julian. Everywhere that he could see, the factory was teeming with satiated cross-genders, working effectively.

"When do you plan to increase the size of your company Julie?" asked Martin.

"May be in the next year uncle. What do you say dad?" said Julian.

"When the director decides something in a company, who am I to say anything in protest?" said Joe and ducked under the table as a small pillow came sailing towards him from Julian.

"Well Julie dear, would you happen to have a seat vacant? I have a candidate for the post of a manager for your next plant" said Martin with a wry smile.

"Who is it uncle? Anyone you name is going to be the manager of the whole plant with immediate effect."

"Martin, your uncle"

"You know that mine is only for people like me... special people" said Julian with a merry smile.

"Why do you think Joe came to *me* for help regarding you in the first place Julie? I am not your *uncle* baby. I am your *aunt Marty*" said Martin.

Julian looked at Joe who nodded his head. Julian jumped from his chair and hugged Martin with a bear hug that bound them with an everlasting bond.

THE RED BALL

I hated crowds.

I would suffocate in a taxi when the driver was present. I was horrified at the idea of travelling in a local bus. As for trains, the mere thought made me want to throw up. I avoided going to office along the common routes and took the most circuitous one, mostly devoid of humans. Tuticorin was not a metropolitan city. Yet, it had enough of my species to make me claustrophobic. I was relaxed for the past month or so, with my office on leave. That gave me the perfect reason to be holed up in my room, with my daughter.

My daughter learnt the art of picking up a ball and throwing it, just a month back. It was glorious, to see a bundle of flesh plodding after a ball with giggles and all sorts of sounds – most of which I could not understand, but loved. You know, she had a special look for me. The tone of her voice when she called me *appa* differed from the tone she used for other people. We bonded over the ball game, much like how my classmates said they had gotten close with one another over cricket. So this must be the feeling, I thought dreamily when her voice cut in, "*appa thaa, appa thaa*," meaning 'give the ball, dad.' I flicked the ball towards her with my forefinger.

An incident that day changed the course of my life, and that of my daughter. We were playing 'throw and catch,' my daughter and I. The front doors of my house were made of steel grille. There were two doors which could be slid from the sides to the centre and then secured with a lock, a common feature in South Indian houses. The left door was open and the right closed. The ball sped out of my room and landed on the verandah. I came running, to see the ball bouncing out of the open door to the street.

To my utter discomfiture a dog rushed up, caught the ball in its mouth and ran off. It was a common Indian mongrel, the likes of which can be seen on almost all Indian streets, and tough to single out. To retrieve the ball, tougher... The toughest would be to go out among people, brush against them if necessary and worst of all, give reasons as to why I, of all people, was on the streets... I could feel the hair on my hands and legs standing straight at the thought.

"Did you have to keep the door open at this time?" I shouted.

"So you remember that there is another room in this house! Do you realize that you have come out of your room after five days?" my wife retorted.

"Didn't I tell you that my office is closed?"

"Don't you have a wife? What do you consider me? A maid? At the least, can't you sit and talk with me?" came a volley of questions.

This was too much for me. I retreated to the sanctuary of my room. Peace reigned for a minute.

"*Appa*, ball *thaa*..." came a demanding voice near me.

I glanced up from my mobile to see my daughter looking at me expectantly.

"My *kuttyma* wants a ball? Wait... Dad will get one for you" I said, getting up from my mat. I went to the corner where her toys were heaped on the floor and searched for the multicoloured ball that she loved. I returned with the ball, cleaning it with my tee-shirt.

"Here you are baby. Come on. Let's play with this ball" I said.

She set up a wail that would have been heard for miles, making my wife come running from the kitchen. The little girl stood pointing at the ball and refused to stop her cries. What she said through her sobbing was difficult to decipher.

"Red ball" said the little one. "Red ball" she repeated amidst her cries.

"She knows red?" I shouted in surprise.

"My mother taught her" my wife replied bluntly.

"Here, *kuttyma...* let's play with this ball. I will get you a red ball in the evening" I said, trying to placate her.

"Ignore her for the time being. She will forget the ball in a while" said my wife, bringing the vegetable cutter and some beans into the living room.

The crescendo of my daughter's cries increased. I swept her up in my arms and took her to the book shelf, trying to change the scenario. I found it strange that the usually amicable Mickey and Minnie had turned despicable to her. All that she wanted was a red ball. And I couldn't find a replacement. What was more disconcerting was the smirk that played around the corners of my wife's mouth.

This left me with the inevitable. Someone had to go out and buy a ball. And *that someone* was me. The oppressive feeling of going to a crowded shop came upon me heavily. I looked pleadingly at my wife as I had done in all the other occasions before, but an iron curtain had been drawn across.

"Do you think Murugan *Anna*'s shop will have a red ball?" I asked, a wild hope flaring in my heart. The shop was at the corner of my street. I need not walk for a long distance or meet many people. Furthermore, Murugan knew of my predicament and never asked unnecessary questions.

My wife's answer snubbed the spark of hope that lit up.

"Murugan runs a grocery shop" she replied with a chuckle that made me want to bang my head against the wall. 'Should've observed the shop,' I cursed myself. She continued, her words dripping sarcasm, "Do you know that today is the twenty second of May, 2018?"

"Yes... I know. Why?" I asked, thrown off-balance by this sudden question, but wary.

"Just to know if you are on this earth mentally too" she replied.

I said no more, but deposited my girl gently into my wife's hands, re-tied my *lungi* securely and made for the grille. The moment I stepped out of the door I could feel a difference in the street. People stood in groups. Big groups! Unusual! I panicked. Would they strike conversation with me? What should I answer them? I steeled my heart and moved on. None seemed to pay any attention to me. As I left my street and walked to the main road, intending to go to a supermarket there, I found to my dismay that the shop was locked. I had to cross two more streets to go to the next shop. It was then that I heard the noise, akin to the rumbling of thunder. It got closer.

As I stood wondering, from around the bend on the main road came a group of people, shouting slogans such as "Down with Sterlite... shut down Sterlite..." The shouts became louder as more groups joined in. A young girl kept shouting animatedly, "We need clean air," which was taken up by the people around. *So, the protest has become big,* I thought. This was the reason my office had been shut for some days. I understood then, the reason for the rumbling sound. The crowd was approximately twenty thousand in strength. It was a motley crowd of elderly people supported by middle aged sons and relatives, mothers with their toddlers and infants, and youth, of all sexes, in their prime of power and courage.

I wished the ground would swallow up and cover me. My knees refused to support me. As I searched for support, I noticed the steps of a closed shopping complex. I sat down on the steps and buried my face between my knees. The noise kept increasing. I looked up. The road was not visible. As far as I could see, it was a sea of human heads.

"Come, we will sit here" said a female voice. I turned to see a young mother standing with her daughter and son. The son gave me a smile that forced me to reciprocate – a first for me.

"I want lemon rice" said the boy, to his mother.

"You will eat what I give. I cannot prepare a different variety for everyone in the house." So saying she handed over a tiffin box to the boy, who opened it reluctantly. The girl had meanwhile started munching on the *upma* from her box.

The boy gave me a forlorn look on seeing the food in his box. I looked uneasily. He kept looking at me, hoping perhaps that I could be his saviour. "Hmmm... *Upma* is good for health" I managed to stammer. His look turned outright hostile.

"Eat quickly. We have to go" said the mother impatiently, pushing a water bottle into her daughter's mouth.

The mother gave me a warm smile and asked, "Aren't you joining the protest?"

"No *akka*..." I said, and noticing her strange look added hastily, "I mean, yes *akka*. I am just taking a breather." She smiled. "Sterlite must be closed. I want clean air for my children."

"Yes *akka*," I nodded.

"You have children?"

"Yes, yes... a daughter... she is two now."

I watched the family move off, mingling with the crowd. Strangely, for the first time in my life, I dared to do the same. I became part of the human flood walking for the sake of their children and their city. As I came to a bend I saw to my delight that a petty shop was open, supplying water to the people. But what caught my attention was a hanging net bulging with balls of various colours. I pushed my way through the throng and reached the shop.

"Anna, do you have a red ball?" I asked.

"Ball? I do not have time to check. Here... check inside this net" said the shopkeeper, and continued supplying water and buttermilk to the passing people. I searched. To my dismay, there was no red ball. It was then that sounds of distortion, anger and fear wafted through the air. I strained to see what was happening. I could see black smoke rising from the distance. Sharp blasts, similar to tyres being ruptured, echoed. People fled in all directions. I looked around, stupefied. The shopkeeper shouted at me.

"Run *thambi*... run... they are shooting... save your life." So saying he ran from the place. Before I realized, I was running like hell, my legs pounding with pain. There was something in my hand. It was a white, fist-sized sponge ball from the shop. I made a mental note to repay the man later. I could see police jeeps and vans coming from all directions. There was a police van that had a dark and burly policeman on the top. In his hands was a rifle, its long barrel pointed at the crowd. His yellow jersey made him stand out. Without any hesitation, he fired into the running crowd. A cry rose up. There was no place to hide. The plains near the roads were full of police. And in the fleeing crowd, I saw the boy, the *upma* eating one who had sat near me some time back. He was running as fast as his tender legs could carry him. His mother and sister were nowhere in sight.

It was then that I saw something that sent shivers down my spine. The boy crossed a road and ran. I followed him. A Hero Honda Splendor came on the scene and slowed down. The man on the back pulled out a revolver and sent a shot towards the scattered people, in the direction of the boy. The shot was mistimed and the bullet went whistling in the air. How could a civilian shoot at the crowd, thought I? Then I realized... policemen in plain clothes... but why? That too firing to kill, at a peaceful crowd! Something was amiss.

I dived at the boy and rolled along with him. I saw that he was crying. I held him firmly and shouted, "Be still boy. Don't move." He kept still, too scared to move. People were still running around. I raised my head slowly. The bike was nowhere in sight. I took the boy by his hands and we started running together. I felt something hit me from behind. My legs felt tired and wooden. The boy felt the tug at his hands as I slowed down. "You keep running... I will escape." He hesitated, rubbing the tears from his face. "Go boy... go. Do not stop... till you reach... home," I gasped. The boy moved out of sight as I fell down.

The newspapers were filled with news of the brutal killing of civilians by the Police of the Tamil Nadu government. Nine people were killed on the 22nd of May, 2018. But none of the newspapers mentioned the young father who lay dead with a red ball clutched in his hand. On close inspection, it was a white ball, drenched red in his blood.

WATCH OUT

The gentle and steady rain on the lush landscape decked the environment with beauty undisclosed during summer. The dense forests of the Western Ghats thrived and throbbed with the music of the wild. The whooping calls of lion-tailed macaques and the nasal communication of the Rufous Babblers wafted down to the hamlets dotted peacefully on the outskirts of the forest plains. The occasional trumpeting of wallowing elephants caused villagers to pause in their fields and look anxiously. The sole breaker to the peaceful routine of the forests was the deafening gun shots of the English who took refuge under the green canopy, making its inhabitants refugees. The usual visitors were district collectors, captains of different regiments, merchants and doctors – in short, all prominent Englishmen and their families from the Tinnevelly District, located in the southern tip of the Madras Presidency. Being in power, Her Majesty's countrymen faced no opposition from the Indians, but only service akin to worship.

Tinnevelly in 1910 housed more English people than other towns nearby because of the many schools, colleges and businesses that were founded and run by the conquerors. Dohnavur, the biggest village between Tinnevelly and the forest range, was gateway to the sanctuary of the foreigners. Being captain of the watch, it fell on me to ensure order in the village. February was always hectic, with many foreigners preferring the dense forest and its game to the hot and dusty countryside of South India. Half of my men would accompany me to the forest to assist the aristocrats while the rest would manage the village.

That day was no different. The fiery orange ball was dying a slow death, forcing humans to hurry toward their abodes. The patio of the spacious forest rest house beheld some Englishmen lounging on bamboo chairs and smoking Dindigul Cigars, which were later manufactured by Spencer's and became a favourite of Sir Winston Churchill. The ladies and the children were indoors, peals of laughter emanating from the candle lit rooms, denoting the mood inside. Seven of my men and I were huddled under a giant umbrella-shaped tree.

"When are we going home sahib?" a soldier asked.

"Wait for two more days Karuppa. This crowd will go back to Tinnevelly. We can move to our village" said I.

"I miss my wife's *karuvattu kolambu*" said Karuppan, the fatso of my team. His ability to eat and think of food at all times was legendary.

"Sahib, yesterday it was *aattukaal kolambu*, today it is *karuvattu kolambu* and tomorrow it would be some other *kolambu*. Karuppan cannot think of anything else" countered Raja, one of the youngest members of the team.

"Hey Raja...wait till you get married" shouted Karuppan and threw a twig. Raja ducked, and the dry twig broke into several pieces on the steps of the patio.

I got up, cursed Karuppan and ran towards the patio, muttering apologies to the Englishmen. As I cleared the place of the broken wood pieces,

"Put those aside and come in for a while Sergunaam" boomed the stentorian voice of the Headquarters Assistant Collector, Alfred Tampoe.

"Sorry for the disturbance sahib" I said humbly.

"Did I pronounce your name properly this time?" asked Tampoe with a smile. He had had trouble last time pronouncing my name, though he was Ceylonese.

"It is Sargunam sahib."

"Ha ha… these Indian names… well Sergunaam, my friends and I were discussing something which we thought might be made clearer, had you a mind to shed light on it" he said, eyeing me carefully.

"Yes sahib."

"Have you perchance received news of the latest act of burglary in our district?"

"I… have not sahib" I spluttered, quelling the fear rising to my throat. I knew the destination of the conversation and was not overly fond of it.

"Mr. Tampoe, if I may intervene, these locals have no regard for us and our Empire, and will go to any lengths to safeguard the dacoits roaming around these parts. The probability of these dark skinned rats being a part of the heinous act wouldn't surprise me" spat Donovan Harbringer, the European Superintendent of Police, Tinnevelly.

"It is the mark of a gentleman to be courteous at all times, Mr. Harbringer" said Tampoe rising to his feet smoothly and silencing the police with his look. "Now to continue from where we left Sergunaam," said Tampoe, walking out from the patio into the forest, with me following him dutifully. He crossed the tree near which Karuppan and Raja stood bewildered, under the assumption that I was being chastised for their misconduct.

"A week ago, the brigand Jamboo… Jamboo… lee…?" stuttered Tampoe with a confused look on his face.

"Jambulingam sahib" said I, looking at the assistant collector.

"Yes yes…" continued Tampoe impatiently. "He had had the audacity to block the only bus plying between Travancore and Nagerkovil and relieve passengers of their belongings. What has irked the police department is that one of the victims was Ms. Elizabeth Krazer, the love interest of Mr. Donovan Harbringer."

"I am sorry sahib. I did not know…"

"Wait Sergunaam. I am not done yet. Mr. Harbringer went to Nagerkovil to pick up a highly expectant Ms. Krazer. Who he met instead was a cringing Irish lady scared witless by having stared at death in the guise of Jamboo… whatever."

I remained silent.

"We believe the robber paid a visit to your village Sergunaam. He relieved Ms. Krazer of a unique belt made of crocodile skin. It had her fiancé's name inscribed on it. The belt was found today."

"Where sahib?" I asked breathlessly.

Tampoe looked at me searchingly.

"In your village… around the neck of a sheep."

I was at a loss for words. Jambulingam had been known for his

audacity, recklessness, dacoity and helping nature. But this...
this showed that he possessed sense of humour too. And that
was a quality rare in outlaws!

"I want you to find the link between the outlaw and your village
Sergunaam. Remember that I will hold you responsible for
things that happen in your village. Mr. Harbringer's anger is
also to be kept on mind" said Tampoe walking towards the
house, leaving me to my thoughts.

My mind swam back to an incident. Dohnavur's annual sports
meet had been in progress. Winning was a matter of prestige
and honour. The stone lifting competition that regularly
garnered the largest number of spectators was in progress.

As I pushed my way towards the centre, I saw something that
would remain etched in my memory. A young man was bent
over a mammoth stone on the ground. I saw his broad
shoulders and back bulge with muscles as he lifted the stone.
His neck heaved and calves tightened. He held the stone close
to his enormous chest and walked... fifteen steps amidst the
roaring applause and unbelief of the audience who had never
imagined such a feat possible.

The record before this had been a mere three step walk!

Jambulingam had risen from obscurity to popularity overnight.

Men wanted to be like Jambulingam. Women wanted to
possess him. His strength became stuff of folklore. In an act
of greed, an English merchant transferred to his name, land
that did not belong to him. Unfortunately for him,
Jambulingam's land was also annexed illegally. All attempts to
get the wrong righted by Jambulingam were in vain.

Left without a place to stay and jeered at by the English, a lamb became a lion, one that terrorized two districts of the Madras Presidency and was a nightmare to the Royal Police of Travancore. Thereafter none of that merchant's goods reached anywhere but Jambulingam's hideouts. The major disadvantage to the authorities was the unstinting support shown by all villagers, for Jambulingam never robbed from the poor, but stripped bare the English and the rich who were in cahoots with the foreigners, and distributed to all in need.

"Sergunaam" called Tampoe, breaking my reverie.

I hurried to the guest house.

"Make arrangements for us to leave for Tinnevelly tomorrow morning" said Tampoe.

"Yes sahib" I replied, my mind still revolving around Jambulingam.

"You may retire for the night" said Tampoe and walked away. I went to arrange palanquins for the next day's ride.

Four months passed with no news of Jambulingam's act of violence or kindness. The July climate was mild. I was making my patrol one evening when there was an unusual buzz in the market. On top of some stacked up sacks stood a news bearer from the Tinnevelly Magistrate surrounded by youngsters eager for news. On the occasion of the coronation of King George of England, celebrations were arranged in Tinnevelly in November. Robert William Ashe, the District Collector of Tinnevelly was to preside over the function in which games were to be conducted in honour of the King.

I received summons to meet Ashe in Tinnevelly the very next day. He was with Harbringer who eyed me ominously.

"I believe you are aware of the celebrations in November" said the collector, looking down at me from his seat.

"Yes sahib."

"We are sure that the notorious dacoit Jaam…boolee…ngaam would not be able to resist the temptation of trying his skills in games."

"Sure sahib" said I, still unsure as to why he had sent for me.

"You will assist Harbringer in identifying the robber. He will do the rest" said the collector, twirling his dense moustache.

"I swear by King George to break all the bones of that ruffian" growled Harbringer.

November came in a rush. Ashe was escorted by officers in six elephants, three leading and three following. He was resplendent, seated on an elephant that was decked with gold. Booming guns welcomed the procession entering the playground of St. John's College. Ashe, Tampoe and officials from the other districts of the Madras Presidency took seats on a raised dais. Ashe talked of the might of the British Empire. Rich and fat Indians who had managed to secure seats on stage clapped the loudest after his speech.

The games were soon underway. The public stood behind ropes tied to stakes that were driven into the ground. My men stood next to the stage, with Harbringer having constant eye contact with me. Each unknown contestant's entry made his head to swivel in my direction. The wrestling competition brought the loudest cheers from the spectators. A lad from Shencottah remained unbeaten till the end, managing to get wide appreciation.

There was erected on the ground, between the huge stage and the public, two makeshift doors, their frames planted firmly, parallel to each other. Ten feet beyond the doors were placed two stones of equal weight. The participants had to lift the stone, walk through the door and place the stone in front of the stage. There was a gap of almost twenty feet between the stage and the door. I stood immobile watching the crowd encourage the participants. None could lift the stone. Walking with it seemed out of the question.

An English soldier detached himself from his companions and came near the stage.

There was an announcement.

"Citizens of the Indian Colony of the Great British Empire, we present, on behalf of the Crown, Steeler, the undisputed champion. If there is anyone who can lift the stone and walk through the door towards the stage farther than Steeler goes, great would be the reward."

There was a great stir among the audience. Harbringer looked warily at the crowd, looking for potential Jambulingams.

"Is there no opponent from the Indian Colony? Are there no strong men to contest?" shouted the announcer.

Blood boiled. But none dared step out. The stones were huge and Steeler was gigantic. Steeler began his walk towards the stone.

I observed him carefully as he walked to the door. I knew that time was running out but suppressed the urge to check my watch. I took a deep breath and started counting in reverse under my breath. "Ten, nine, eight, seven..."

"Isn't there any male from your pitiless country? This shows the might of..."

The words were cut short as a fierce war cry rose close to me. Karuppan, the fatso of my watch stepped out of line and walked towards the stone. Steeler paused, turned and watched. The crowd sent a deafening roar. I was glad that Karuppan decided to save India's face.

The contestants stripped to the waist. While Steeler bowed towards the stage, Karuppan looked defiantly. Both bent and assessed the stones. Steeler was the first to get up. The English sent up a cry of triumph as he started his walk towards the door. Karuppan gave a grunt that was lost in the shouts of the crowd and lifted the stone. Hugging the stone, he walked towards the door, his eyes on the figure of Steeler receding through the door.

The air was electrified as Steeler crossed the door and managed ten more tottering steps towards the stage. The blue veins on his hands snaked all the way up to his temples, his face a deep crimson. Grimacing due to the weight of the slipping stone, he dropped it and stood panting. All eyes were now on Karuppan who too had crossed the door. He was a mass of black muscle. His colour did not betray his efforts. His veins were not prominent. Yet, he came on. The crowd went berserk with joy.

Karuppan then did something totally unexpected. He drew parallel to Steeler who watched him open mouthed and asked,

"Need help?"

The colossus then adjusted the stone, walked till the stage and dropped the stone in front of the flabbergasted Englishmen.

All this without showing visible sign of effort!

Ashe and Harbringer went pale. Tampoe smiled. A piece of land was written to the name of Karuppan. The dignity and honour of India was saved, with England witnessing it. As for the English authorities who bayed for the blood of Jambulingam, I must say they were disappointed in not capturing him. The fact was, though they saw Jambulingam, they did not recognize him.

For, how could I have betrayed my country and told them that Karuppan of my watch was Jambulingam!

A TALE OF FRIENDSHIP

"I wish I could turn back the clock and bring the wheels of time to a stop" sighed my grandmother.

"Why grandma? What was so special about the past?" I asked.

"Everything my love, everything" replied my grandma, adjusting herself in the rocking chair, her scarf billowing in the wind and threatening to come off her angular chin. Her flaming red hair, once famous among the Dutch and the British East Indian Colonies, though having lost some colour, was still lustrous to look. The mix of grey hair gave her a regal composure. Yet, at the mention of the days past, she looked girlish, her eyes twinkling, merry lines forming at the corners of her eyes and mouth. I looked down at the dense grove of trees surrounding the Udayagiri fort and wondered what could've been better than this beautiful coastal town with its gentle climate, rich flora and hardworking natives. Strong and sweet smell of ripe jackfruit filled the air, intoxicating.

The sound of waves lapping on the sea shore was music to my ears. Having a grandfather who was a naval commander and a father who took after him ensured that the descendant did not disappoint. I took to sea like an otter does. Having lived the major part of my 15 years on the seas with my father, I found it strange to feel solid ground beneath my feet for more than three months at a stretch. Looking contently at the sea in the distance, I sipped tea from a copper cup, a servant standing nearby with a copper jug, ready to replenish when necessary. The steady drizzle had drenched the landscape, hushing the otherwise humming forest.

"The one who made all the difference was Ananthapadmanabhan, your grandfather's friend" smiled granny.

"Ananthapadmanabhan? A friend? But grandma, everyone says he was an enemy of grandpa!" I blurted out.

"No honey. I'll tell you who he was" replied grandma.

"With voices… with voices…" I piped in. It meant that she had to tell the story as it happened, by mimicking each character individually. Grandma smiled sweetly, patted me on the head and began.

It was 1727.

Marthandan could hardly believe his luck. To have glimpsed the fleeing animal within half-a-day's hunt was nothing short of a miracle. This will be a fine tale to tell King Rama Varma, thought Marthandan, as he galloped furiously beneath the densely populated trees. His fresh horse thundered along, its legs hardly seeming to touch the surface. Slowly but inexorably, the prince pulled away from fellow hunters and guards, his horse powering him close to the prey. In his excitement, Marthandan failed to notice the big cat slowing down. When realization dawned on him, Marthandan reined in his horse, only to come face to face with the huge tiger that had turned, and was measuring him with hostility. The prince understood the reason. Drummers were closing in from other sides, forcing the tiger onto the path of the hunters.

Marthandan knew that this was his moment. He would either carry the skin and claws of the tiger to the palace or be dead meat within minutes. He hefted his spear slowly and carefully, extending his hand back for the throw, when his horse reared up, landing him unceremoniously on the slippery ground. He looked up to see the tiger hunching itself for the leap and the spear that now lay a foot away from him. The tiger leaped, and let out an ear-splitting roar mid-way. An arrow jutted from its side. The leap faltered and the tiger landed awkwardly some distance away. It roared in pain and turned to face the new danger.

Marthandan rolled over quickly and picked up his spear. There was a hissing sound and another arrow tore into the neck of the tiger. Maddened with rage and not knowing the whereabouts of the new enemy, the tiger leaped upon the crouching prince. But by now, Marthandan was prepared. He met the onslaught by kneeling down, the butt of his spear held firmly to the ground, and the sharp, jagged end pointing upwards. The tiger closed down on Marthandan, never to get up. The force of the charge carried the spear right through its large neck. The other hunters came on time to see their prince crawl from under the impaled body of the tiger, his face and body bruised and bleeding profusely. His clothing was discoloured by the moist red soil, giving him a disheveled appearance.

"My lord, my lord, are you safe?" shouted a couple of guards, jumping from their horses and rushing towards the heir to the throne of Travancore.

"I am alive…" said Marthandan, evidently shaken by the near death experience. Remembering the arrows, he looked around to trace the archer who had saved him.

A young man of about Marthandan's age climbed down from a tamarind tree. The newcomer's quick breathing made the scars on his bare chest writhe in response, making them seem alive. Uncertainty was writ large on his self.

"Ah, my friend… thanks for the timely help" smiled Marthandan, looking at the youngster. The dark young man smiled nervously at him

in return, bowed low and said, "My lord, I believe I have spoiled your hunt by shooting my arrows uninvited. I thought your life was in danger."

"My life was indeed in danger. If not for you, I might probably be a mangled mass of blood and sinews" said Marthandan, and added swiftly, "May I know your origin?"

"I am the son of Perumal Asan, my lord. I have seen you once in the palace when I came with my Asan" replied the youth meekly.

"That brings us close then...meet me in the palace tomorrow. I will take you to King Rama Varma, my uncle" said Marthandan, mounting his horse.

He gave a cursory glance at the carcass and slapped the rump of the horse, speeding away into the vast greenery of the forest, leaving the remains of the tiger to be brought to the palace by his guards.

"Who is that young man grandma?" I interjected, unable to contain my curiosity.

"Shhh... Eustace, you mustn't disturb the flow of the story" reprimanded my grandmother, and seeing my forlorn face added with a gentle smile, "No more interruptions, my dear..."

She bade a native give me some jackfruit pips on a banana leaf. As I took one, she smiled and said, "That young man was Ananthapadmanabhan."

Ananthapadmanabhan moved away from the dead tiger and the palace guards deep into the forest of Attingal. He had just saved the heir prince from impending death! He shivered as he thought about the impulse with which he had acted. Danger or death, no one was allowed to interfere in

Royal matters. However, the prince was pleased. The thought gave Padmanabhan undue joy.

King Rama Varma was pleased with Padmanabhan for saving his nephew, the heir, and made him the companion of Prince Marthandan, much to the consternation of the King's sons. They were not happy with the youngster whose father was the head of 108 martial arts centres throughout the kingdom of Travancore. Needless to say, Ananthapadmanabhan was an expert in martial warfare.

"But grandma, when the King had sons, how can his nephew be the heir to the throne?" I asked, having dutifully gulped down two plates of juicy jackfruit pips, and longing for more.

Grandma didn't mind the interruption this time. She rather looked at me like a teacher clarifying the doubt of a student. She said, "The rule of Travancore states that only nephews of kings can become kings, Eustace. That cannot be changed; hence Prince Marthandan."

"Ok grandma… but how did Ananthapadmanabhan meet grandpa?" I asked again.

My grandma looked down at me, rustled my hair and said, "always in a hurry… just like your Dad. Let me skip a few incidents and come to that part… and before I continue… one more interference, I stop the narration."

She tried her best to look at me strictly and almost succeeded when a crow that whizzed past dropped a half-rotten mouse on her lap. She gave a gasp that turned into a seemingly never ending high pitched scream, and flayed her arms in all possible directions. I feared she might sprout wings and fly from the ramparts. Her actions finally reaped fruits and the decomposed rat landed some distance away. I strove to maintain a straight face. After a few heartbeats, we happened to look at each other at the same time, breaking into uncontrollable peals of laughter that made the guards down below us, at the fort's entrance, to look up.

Finally, she sobered up, made a sign at me to be quiet and began again.

It was 1739.

The then Prince Marthandan was now called Marthanda Varma, for he was the King of Travancore. He had transformed himself into a battle-king, annexing small fiefdoms and kingdoms around him to his expanding Kingdom. Though hard pressed internally and externally, he always managed to come out victorious.

Kottarakara was a fiefdom under the patronage of the Dutch East Indian Company. It's annexation by Marthandan forced Gustaaf Van Imhoff, the Dutch governor of Ceylon, to meet him in person.

"What does Travancore have to do with Kottarakara?" asked Imhoff.

"Let not the governor talk about things that do not concern him" replied Marthandan hotly.

"This would force the Dutch forces into Travancore" threatened Imhoff.

"I have always considered an invasion of Europe. Do you suggest that I start with Holland?" said Marthandan, his voice sepulchral.

It was early February, 1741.

Imhoff made the Princess of Kottarakara the ruler of the kingdom, much against the threat of Maharaja Marthanda Varma. The King sent word for Ananthapadmanabhan.

"I am moving north with the army. Ramayyan Dalawa is leading our regiment. Keep the Kingdom safe here."

"I will my lord" replied Padmanabhan.

It was late July, 1741.

Ananthapadmanabhan was taking a stroll as usual in the forests near Colachel, an important trading town of the Kingdom of Travancore. A rustling sound made him look upwards. He glanced up to see a Malabar giant squirrel take a leap from one tree. He stood transfixed as the brown squirrel spread all its legs, its skin near the cream coloured legs taut. He could see the distinct white spot between its ears as the squirrel sailed above him and landed five trees farther from where he stood. It was followed by no less than 100 squirrels, all of them gracefully clearing the trees and disappearing under the canopy of trees. He was all admiration for Nature's wonder when a conch sounded in his mind.

Malabar giant squirrels generally rest mid-day and are active early morning hours and evenings. It was mid-day.

Something was amiss!

He ran to his horse, untied it expertly while jumping on the steed, displaying stunning equestrian skills as he sped towards Kalkulam, the capital of Travancore. As he neared the town of Colachel, he understood the grave danger the Kingdom was in, and the reason for the migration of the squirrels. He could hear loud explosions. He was in time to see three men-of-war pounding the buildings near the coast. The sails carried the insignia of the Dutch East India Company, a big V at the centre, with O written on the left leg and C on the right. The letter 'A' was on top of 'V' to denote Amsterdam.

Padmanabhan rode like a demented warrior to Kalkulam. He did not want the trade-rich town of Colachel to become cannon fodder of the Dutch. At the same time, he had vowed to protect the capital. He stationed his army, with cannons and guns, on the beach of Colachel. The pigeons of Marthanda Varma were speeding towards their owner with news of the invasion.

Eustachius De Lannoy was the commander of the Dutch forces that invaded Colachel. After pounding some structures near Colachel, the ships anchored there, displaying a show of strength. The dusk of the third day saw the war ships move towards the port of Colachel. What met De Lannoy's eyes shocked him. On the beach stood an army numbering thousands. To add to the plight of the Dutch, there were cannons directed towards the sea. Once the ships came into range, they would be blown to smithereens. The Indians using artillery was unbelievable.

The shock was much too heavy for De Lannoy. But he was no coward. He chose another route and by the next morning, the Dutch forces had landed and were on their way to Kalkulam. Marthandan and Ramayyan marched overnight with the Travancore's army to halt the advance of De Lannoy towards Kalkulam. Caught between two armies, the foxy De Lannoy retreated to a spot near Colachel.

Padmanabhan welcomed Marthandan in Kalkulam, as the army rested.

"I have kept the Kingdom safe, as promised lord" bowed Padmanabhan.

"But what of the town of Colachel? De Lannoy would have ravaged the town on his way to Kalkulam" replied Marthandan, concern for his subjects creasing his noble face.

"My army is stationed on the beach of Colachel, my lord. That forced De Lannoy to use the forest route to reach Kalkulam. Colachel is safe" smiled Ananthapadmanabhan.

"Army? Yours? I took all our soldiers with me Padmanabha! What are you talking about?" asked the astonished monarch, twirling his moustache. Ramayyan Dalawa looked annoyed. He did not favour Ananthapadmanabhan's proximity to the King.

"Let us first defeat De Lannoy. I will show you my lord" replied Padmanabhan.

As Marthandan's army marched out of Kalkulam after the retreating De Lannoy, Ananthapadmanabhan rode at the head of the cavalry division from Tinnevelly, fighting for Marthandan. The King and Ramayyan Dalawa headed the infantry division.

The battle was short-lived.

The Dutch counted on the strength of its artillery, whereas the Kingdom of Travancore was fighting for its country, and had superior numbers. As the Dutch opened fire, arrows tore into the Dutch ranks from the Indians. Shouting their war cry of 'Adi Kollu, Adi Kollu,' the infantry kept advancing steadily despite the front line faltering initially.

So engrossed were De Lannoy's troops in the melee that they failed to notice the cavalry charging from behind, till the thundering of hoofs bore down on them. The battle became a rout. De Lannoy, his lieutenant Donadi and 24 officers were captured by Ananthapadmanabhan.

It was a proud moment for Padmanabhan as De Lannoy and his officers were brought before him. Mistaking Padmanabnan for Marthandan, De Lannoy laid down his arms and knelt down before anyone could realize.

"I, De Lannoy, the Chief Naval Commander of the Dutch East India Company, surrender myself and my forces to you without any conditions and demands, oh Maharaja Marthanda Varma!"

Everyone was stunned. Padmanabhan responded at once.

"Rise up, Commander De Lannoy. I am not Maharaja Marthandan, but Ananthapadmanabhan Nadar, the Commander of the Maharaja's Cavalry" said he, motioning Lannoy to rise up.

Ten minutes later De Lannoy was kneeling in front of the King. After the surrender Marthandan thanked De Lannoy for not sacking the villages between Colachel and Kalkulam.

"But Maharaja, how could I sack them? Your vast regiments in the beach of Colachel made us take another route" said Lannoy.

"Regiments? On the beach?" Marthandan wondered aloud.

He turned at once to see Padmanabhan smiling.

"Please come with me Lord" he said, and with Ramayyan Dalawa tailing along, the trio rode to the beach of Colachel.

There stood thousands of soldiers, with guns. Moving closer, Marthandan took a sharp intake of breath and stood rooted to the spot. Thousands of oars were dug in the ground, with earthen pots kept at the top. On each oar rested another slanting oar. From a distance, the beach looked armed to the teeth for war, with gun-wielding soldiers ready for battle. Added to these were some hundreds of look-alike cannons devised from cut coconut trees.

Marthandan threw to the winds royal tradition and embraced Padmanabhan, much to the discomfiture of Ramayyan.

"I just did what you asked me to do sire" said Ananthapadmanbhan in the European style.

Ministers wanted De Lannoy killed. But Padmanabhan insisted that he be pardoned. Marthandan, in a show of generosity and goodwill made

De Lannoy train the soldiers of Travancore in the European manner, with artillery and firearms. Lannoy's training produced extremely trained regiments who later became a force to reckon with, in safeguarding the fate of Travancore against Tipu Sultan.

De Lannoy was forever grateful for the kind words spoken by Padmanabhan. As for the friendship that was forged between them, the forest warfare and martial art that Padmanabhan taught Lannoy, and the use of guns that De Lannoy taught him, the construction of various forts by Lannoy… they are stories for another day.

"I wish I get a friend in India" said I, smiling broadly. I had taken a liking to Padmanabhan.

"I do hope so, my dear. The Indians are friendly" said my grandma. "Pray you get a friend like Ananthapadmanabhan" she added.

The fort, also called *Dillanai Kotta* by locals in fond remembrance of De Lannoy, witnessed the burial of my grandfather in the fort's church.

"I will get *my* Ananthapadmanabhan, grandma" said I.

The church bell struck. I smiled. My grandma had tears.

GLOSSARY

Akka – Elderly sister

Anna – Elderly brother

Appa – Father

Kuttyma – Beloved

Lungi – A loose garment worn by men of Tamil Nadu

Thaa – Give

Thambi – Younger brother

Tupi – The skull cap used by Muslims in Bangladesh

Upma – A breakfast made using Sooji

HISTORY

The Banana Leaf

The **Rohingya genocide** is a series of ongoing persecutions by the Myanmar government against the Muslim Rohingya people which consists of two phases, the first of which began in October 2016 and ended in January 2017 and the second of which began in August 2017 and is ongoing as of now. The crisis has forced over a million Rohingyas to flee to neighboring countries, most of whom have fled to Bangladesh with others going to India, Thailand, Malaysia and other parts of South and Southeast Asia. The largest wave of Rohingyas to flee Myanmar occurred in 2017 and it resulted in the largest human exodus in Asia since the Vietnam War. The 2016 military crackdown on the Rohingya people has drawn criticism from the UN (which cited possible "crimes against humanity," the human rights group Amnesty International, the U. S. Department of State, the government of neighboring Bangladesh, and the government of Malaysia (where many Rohingya refugees have fled). The Myanmar leader and State Counsellor (*de facto* head of government) and Nobel Peace Prize laureate Aung San Suu Kyi has particularly been criticized for her inaction and silence over the issue and for doing little to prevent military abuses. Under her leadership, Myanmar has also drawn criticism for prosecutions of journalists.

In late 2016 Myanmar's armed forces and police started a major crackdown on Rohingya people in Rakhine State in the country's northwestern region. The Burmese military have been accused of ethnic cleansing and genocide by various United Nations agencies, International Criminal Court officials, human rights groups, journalists, and governments including the United States. The UN has found evidence of wide-scale human rights violations, including extrajudicial killings; gang rapes; arson of Rohingya villages, businesses, and schools; and infanticides, which the Burmese government dismisses as "exaggerations."

Using statistical extrapolations based on surveys conducted with a total of 3,321 Rohingya refugee households in Cox's Bazar, Bangladesh, a study estimated in January 2018 that during the genocide, the military and the local Rakhine Buddhists killed at least 24,000 Rohingya people, gang rapes and other forms of sexual violence against 18,000 Rohingya Muslim women and girls, 116,000 Rohingya were beaten, and 36,000 Rohingya were thrown into fire.

The military drive also displaced a large number of Rohingya people, spurring a refugee crisis. According to UN reports, as of September 2018, over 700,000 Rohingya people had fled or had been driven out of Rakhine state who then took shelter in the neighboring Bangladesh as refugees. In December 2017, two Reuters' journalists who had been covering the Inn Din massacre event were arrested and imprisoned. Foreign Secretary Myint Thu told reporters Myanmar is prepared to accept 2,000 Rohingya refugees from camps in Bangladesh in November 2018.

The 2017 persecution against the Rohingya Muslims and non-Muslims has also been termed as ethnic cleansing and genocide by various UN agencies, ICC officials, human rights groups, and governments. Former British Prime Minister Theresa May and former United States Secretary of State Rex Tillerson called it "ethnic cleansing" while the French President Emmanuel Macron described the situation as "genocide."

The UN described the persecution as "a textbook example of ethnic cleansing." In late September that year, a seven-member panel of the Permanent Peoples' Tribunal found the Myanmar military and the Myanmar authority guilty of the crime of genocide against the Rohingya and the Kachin minority groups. Suu Kyi was again criticized for her silence over the issue and for supporting the military actions.

Subsequently, in November 2017, the governments of Bangladesh and Myanmar signed a deal to facilitate the return of Rohingya refugees to their native Rakhine state within two months, drawing a mixed response from international onlookers.

In August 2018, the office of the United Nations High Commissioner for Human Rights, reporting the findings of their investigation into the August–September 2017 events, declared that the Myanmar military generals should be tried for genocide. On 24 September 2018, Jeremy Hunt, the British Foreign Secretary, held a meeting with some other foreign ministers on the sideline of the United Nations General Assembly to discuss the crisis in Rohingya.

On 27 September 2018, members of the Canadian Parliament voted unanimously to dispossess Suu Kyi of her honorary Canadian citizenship for the atrocities against Rohingya Muslims.

On 23 January 2020, the International Court of Justice ordered Myanmar to prevent genocidal violence against its Rohingya Muslim minority and preserve evidence of past attacks.

Link: https://en.wikipedia.org/wiki/Rohingya_genocide (Last visited on 17th February, 2020)

The Red Ball

The **Thoothukudi police fire** (also known as
the **Thoothukudi Massacre** or **Sterlite Protest Firing**)
took place on 22 May 2018 in Thoothukudi, Tamil Nadu,
India, when Tamil Nadu Police officers fired into a protest of
20,000 people. The protest was against the Sterlite
Copper factory which is known to have caused
environmental pollution.

Background

Sporadic protests have occurred in Thoothukudi in the
Indian state of Tamil Nadu since 1999, directed against the
Sterlite Copper smelting works. The factory is owned by
Vedanta Limited, a subsidiary of Vedanta
Resources. Protestors oppose soil, water and air
contamination caused by the factory. An epidemiological
study carried out by Tirunelveli Medical College in 2006–07
had found increased prevalence of respiratory diseases and
ear, nose and throat (ENT) morbidity in the 5 km radius of
Sterlite Industries. Their report blamed this on air pollution
caused by the industry, Thermal power plants and
automobiles – such as trucks and heavy vehicles – plying in
this area.

Iron content in the groundwater in the area of the plant has been found to be 17–20 times the allowable limit, causing additional health problems for the population already experiencing higher than average incidence of respiratory diseases. The plant is less than 15 Km from the Gulf of Mannar Biosphere Reserve. More than 2.5 lakh (250,000) people live in the vicinity of the plant.

The Sterlite factory made headlines in 2013 due to an alleged gas leak which was not proven in court. The plant was blamed for health issues observed in the area related to gas leakage. Following the alleged gas leak in March 2013, the then chief minister, the late J. Jayalalithaa, ordered its closure. The company appealed to the National Green Tribunal, which overturned the government order. The state moved the Supreme Court against it, where the petition is still pending. The plant closed on March 27 of 2018, with the company citing a 15-day maintenance process. The Supreme Court ordered the company to pay a 100-crore fine and the factory was temporarily shut down by the pollution regulator.

After Sterlite announced its plans to expand the plant, people around Kumarettiyapuram village protested for more than 100 days. A major protest had been conducted peacefully till March 29, 2018.

Firing

On May 22, 2018, thousands of people began to march to the district collector's office to submit a petition when section 144 was on implementation. When section 144 is on impose more than 4 people gathering is unlawful but an unofficial release said 20,000 people took out a procession towards the district collectorate and the copper plant. The police started shooting against the protesters, without any formal warning. Police intentionally shot in the heads of the protesters.13 protesters were killed including a 17-year old school student, and dozens were injured.

FIRs filed in local police stations claimed that the order to shoot was issued by officers in the rank of deputy tahsildars. Some people pointed out that only Collectors have the authority to issue shooting orders.

The Tamil Nadu government ordered a shutdown of Internet in the entire districts of Tuticorin, Tirunelveli and Kanyakumari for five days after the firing.

Link: https://en.wikipedia.org/wiki/Thoothukudi_massacre (Last visited on 17th February, 2020)

Watch out

History

Born in the state of Travancore, Jambulingam grew up working as a farm-hand, until in his early to mid-twenties he took to the road and became a highwayman along the Travancore-Madras Presidency border, operating mainly in the districts of Kanyakumari and Tinnevelly. He formed a band of desperadoes which, at its height, comprised some twenty to thirty men, notably amongst them, Kasi Nadan, Kalluli Mangan and Doravappa, Jambulingam's right-hand man.

They started by waylaying travellers on the highways between Madras and Travancore, an act in which they were in no small measure helped by the poor policing of the densely forested frontier. Also abetting them was the division of jurisdiction between the British forces in the Presidency and the Royal Police in Travancore.

Jambulingam Nadar's *modus operandi* was to have his gang lay in wait in thickets or copses, signalling each other with owl-hoots or whistles, awaiting unwitting passers-by on foot or on bullock-cart. Upon locating a suitable target they would track them down until a safe opportunity presented itself to ambush them, without risk to themselves. After relieving their victims of their valuables, they would turn their bullocks loose, to give themselves time to get away.

Their fast-growing notoriety brought upon them the unwelcome attention of the law, by the mid-1920s, with the Madras and Travancore police commencing joint patrols of the forests of Aramboly, where Jambulingam was reputed to have his hide-out. Rewards offered for information leading to Jambulingam's capture were to no avail for long, for he maintained the favour of the villagers and peasants by parcelling out his loot with them.

However, c. 1926-'27, information was provided to the Madras Police by one of Jambulingam's gang-members, which led to his being surprised near Aramboly and shot in the act of making his escape. While Doravappa attempted to continue their nefarious work, he was captured by the police in a short while. The gang disbanded soon thereafter.

Link: https://en.wikipedia.org/wiki/Jambulingam_Nadar (Last visited on 17th February, 2020)

A Tale of Friendship

The **Battle of Colachel** (or **Battle of Kulachal**) was fought between the Indian kingdom of Travancore and the Dutch East India Company, during the Travancore-Dutch War. Travancore, under Raja Marthanda Varma, defeated the Dutch East India Company. The defeat of the Dutch by Travancore is considered the earliest example of an organised power from Asia overcoming European military technology and tactics. The Dutch never recovered from the defeat and no longer posed a large colonial threat to India.

In the early 18th century, the Malabar Coast region of present-day Kerala was divided among several small chiefdoms. In the 1730s, Marthanda Varma, the ruler of Travancore, adopted an expansionist policy, and conquered several territories from these small states. This threatened the interests of the Dutch East India Company's command at Malabar, whose spice trade depended on procurement of spices from these states. Marthanda Varma and his vassals refused to honour the monopoly contracts that the Dutch had with the states annexed by Travancore, adversely affecting the Dutch trade in Malabar.

In January 1739, Gustaaf Willem van Imhoff, the Dutch Governor of Ceylon, visited Kochi, and in a July 1739 report, he recommended military action to save the Dutch business in Malabar. Later that year, the Dutch organised an alliance of the rulers of Kochi, Thekkumkur, Vadakkumkur, Purakkad, Kollam, and Kayamkulam. Van Imhoff personally met Marthanda Varma to negotiate peace, threatening to wage war against Travancore if the Dutch terms were not accepted, but Marthanda Varma dismissed the threat, and replied that he had been thinking about invading Europe someday.

In late 1739, the Dutch command at Malabar declared war on Travancore, without obtaining permission or waiting for reinforcements from Batavia. The Dutch deployed a detachment of soldiers from Ceylon against Travancore, under the command of Captain Johannes Hackert. They and their allies achieved several military successes in the initial campaign. In November 1739, the allied army forced the Travancore army stationed near Kollam to retreat, and advanced up to Tangasseri. The British East India Company chief at Anchuthengu congratulated the Dutch on their victory, and requested them to leave the English establishment at Edava in peace. Later, the English also contributed 150 soldiers and ammunition to the Dutch campaign.

By early December 1739, the Dutch and their allies marched towards Attingal and Varkala. When the Travancore army withdrew to check an invasion by Chanda Sahib of Arcot in the south, the allies achieved further military successes. However, the Dutch decided to wait for reinforcements from Ceylon before waging further war against Travancore.

The Dutch wanted to take advantage of this situation, but they were unable to receive reinforcements from Batavia because of the riots there. In November 1740, the Dutch command in Malabar received two small reinforcements of 105 and 70 soldiers from Ceylon, and launched a second campaign against Travancore, resulting in the battle of Colachel.

Surrender of the Dutch

On 5 August 1741, a cannonball fired by the Travancore army fell into a barrel of gunpowder inside the Dutch garrison, and the resulting fire destroyed the entire rice supply of the stockade. Consequently, the Dutch were forced to surrender on 7 August 1741. While the Dutch records mention the date of the surrender as 7 August, some later sources give different dates for the Dutch surrender:

The court chronicle (*Rajyakaryam Churuna*) of Marthanda Varma simply states the date as Āḍi 916 ME, without mentioning any specific day. Historian A. P. Ibrahim Kunju takes the Dutch date (7 August 1741 CE) to be correct.

The Dutch soldiers at Colachel surrendered on the condition that they would be allowed to go to Kanyakumari with their weapons. However, Marthanda Varma did not honour the agreement, and imprisoned them as soon as they came out of the fort. The Travancore forces captured a large number of muskets and some cannons from the Dutch garrison at Colachel. They imprisoned 24 Europeans and several native Christians, who were imprisoned at the Udayagiri Fort in Puliyoorkurichi. Later, Marthanda Varma gave them their weapons back, and asked them to join the Travancore army. Several European prisoners, including Eustachius De Lannoy and Duyvenschot, accepted the offer and served Marthanda Varma.

Link: https://en.wikipedia.org/wiki/Battle_of_Colachel (Last visited on 17th February, 2020)

ABOUT THE AUTHOR

Janneker Lawrence Daniel is a Professor of English, Training and Placement Officer, Soft Skills Trainer and an English Language Trainer. His passion is to transform people through his writing.

He is married, has a daughter he adores and spends his free time restoring motorcycles.

His short stories have been published in various anthologies before. He can be reached at jannekerlawrence@gmail.com.